The Best MOM

CEDAR MILL CO
12505 N
POR

W9-AAY-581

WITHDRAWN
CEDAR MILL LIBRARY

by Sarah Willson
illustrated by Dave Aikins

Ready-to-Read

Simon Spotlight/Nickelodeon
New York   London   Toronto   Sydney

Stephen Hillenburg

Based on the TV series *SpongeBob SquarePants*® created by Stephen Hillenburg
as seen on Nickelodeon®

SIMON SPOTLIGHT

An imprint of Simon & Schuster Children's Publishing Division
1230 Avenue of the Americas, New York, New York 10020

© 2010 Viacom International Inc. All rights reserved. NICKELODEON, *SpongeBob SquarePants*, and all related titles, logos, and characters are
registered trademarks of Viacom International Inc.
All rights reserved, including the right of reproduction in whole or in part in any form.

SIMON SPOTLIGHT, READY-TO-READ, and colophon are registered trademarks of Simon & Schuster, Inc.
For information about special discounts for bulk purchases, please contact Simon & Schuster Special Sales at 1·866·506·1949
or business@simonandschuster.com.
Manufactured in the United States of America
0210 LAK
First Edition
2 4 6 8 10 9 7 5 3 1
Library of Congress Cataloging-in-Publication Data
Willson, Sarah.
The best mom / by Sarah Willson ; illustrated by Dave Aikins. — 1st ed.
p. cm. — (Ready-to-read)
At head of title: Nick SpongeBob SquarePants.
"Based on the TV series SpongeBob SquarePants created by Stephen Hillenburg as seen on Nickelodeon"—T.p. verso.
ISBN 978-1-4169-9675-0
I. Aikins, Dave. II. SpongeBob SquarePants (Television program) III. Title.
PZ7.W6845Bg 2010
[E]—dc22
2009023769

"Cross your fingers, Gary!"
said SpongeBob. "I finished writing
'Why My Mom Is the Best'
for the Kelpo cereal contest."
"Meow!" said Gary.

3

SpongeBob dashed into the
Krusty Krab.
"Sorry I am late, Mr. Krabs!"
he panted. "I just mailed my essay
for a contest about how much
I love my mother. I hope I win!"

Squidward chuckled. "Oh, SpongeBob,
you and your wild and crazy ideas."

"How **much** do you love your mom, eh?" said Mr. Krabs. "That gives me an idea. We will have a special day next week.

Let's see . . . we will call it Take-Your-Mom-to-Lunch Day! Moms will get a penny off their Krabby Patties!"

"Who would take their mom
to **this** dump?" Squidward asked.
"**You** would, if you know what
is good for you," said Mr. Krabs.
"You too, SpongeBob."

Squidward hurried to call his mom.
When SpongeBob called his mom,
she told him that she would not
miss this lunch for the world.

On Take-Your-Mom-to-Lunch Day,
the Krusty Krab was filled with
customers and their moms.

Brrrrring!

Squidward answered the phone.

"It's your mom," he told SpongeBob.

"SpongeBob, dear, I am sorry, but
I cannot make it today,"
said SpongeBob's mom.
"We have bathroom trouble!"

"You . . . you can't?" said SpongeBob
in a tiny voice. "Oh, okay."
He hung up and looked around.
The Krusty Krab was filled with
moms. Everyone's mom—except his.

14

Just then Squidward's mom arrived
at the Krusty Krab.
"Finally you invited me somewhere,"
she grumbled to her son.

Everyone turned to SpongeBob.
"Where is **your** mom?"
asked Mr. Krabs.
"She . . . she can't come,"
said SpongeBob with a sniffle.

"Ha! And I thought you had
the best mom," said Squidward.
"I do!" said SpongeBob.
"Then why isn't she here?"
Squidward asked.

SpongeBob did not want to say
that his mom could not come
because of bathroom trouble.
"She . . . she couldn't come because . . .
she is a famous TV star!"
he blurted out. "And she has to go
somewhere very important in her
big fancy car!"

Squidward rolled his eyes.
Even Mr. Krabs chuckled.
"Whatever you say, SpongeBob,
me boy," he said.

21

Meanwhile at the SquarePants home
SpongeBob's dad had fixed
the problem.
"Oh, good!" said SpongeBob's mom.
"Now I can go to lunch at
the Krusty Krab!"

When SpongeBob's mom opened the
front door, she found a man waiting
for her.

"Congratulations, Mrs. SquarePants!"
he said. "Your son's essay won
the Kelpo cereal contest! **You** are
the best mom! And you win a free
day of beauty!"

"Thank you, that is very nice,
but I do not want a day of beauty."
said SpongeBob's mom. "I just want
to have lunch with my son!"

"Ah, spoken like a true 'best mom,'"
the man said. "We will take you to
your son!"
He led SpongeBob's mom to a
big fancy car.

Back at the Krusty Krab, SpongeBob watched sadly as everyone had lunch with their moms.

"I hope your mom is having
a great time being a TV star,"
Squidward said. "Who knows,
if she has time, she might even
drop by in a big fancy car!"

Just then a big fancy car pulled up
in front of the Krusty Krab.
When the car door opened,
SpongeBob was the first to yell,
"Mom!"

He rushed to hug his mom.
"We will put this on TV!"
said the man.

Squidward's mouth fell open.
"You never take **me** anywhere
in a big fancy car!" snapped his mom.
"Ooh, more customers!" said Mr. Krabs.
"Hurry, Squidward! Quick!
Double the prices!"

"I really do have the best son ever!"
said SpongeBob's mom.
"And I have the best mom ever!"
said SpongeBob.